CREATURE of the WEEK
VOLUME ONE

a coloring book of creepy crawlies,
classic critters, and cultish cryptids

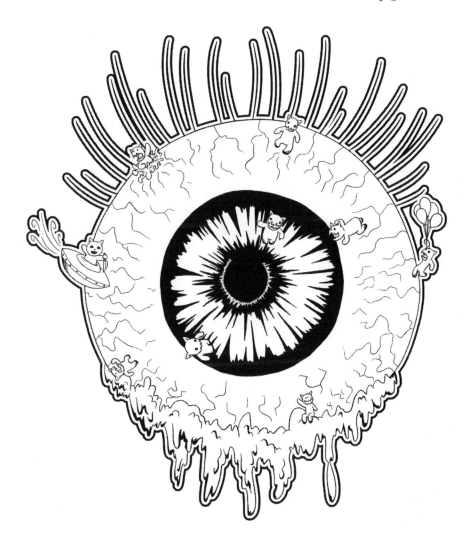

Created by

Donovan Scherer

Creature of the Week
A Coloring Book of Creepy Crawlies, Classic Critters, and Cultish Cryptids

BIGFOOT
BUSINESS SHARK
CHUPACABRA
DANCIN' KRAKEN
GHOST
GRAVEMOTHER
HODAG
JERSEY DEVIL
KRAMPUS
LOCH NESS MONSTER
MARI LWYD
MELVIN
MERMARK
MOTHMAN
MUMMY
NOSFERATU
OLD MAN WINTER
PIZZA OF BADNESS
PIZZA OF GOODNESS
PUGGERFLY
PUMPKIN KID
SALAMBEAU
SANDWITCH
SANTATHULHU
SHRUNKEN HEADS
S'MORES
SPRING BABBY
TACO DOG
THE MOON
TOOTH FAIRY IMPOSTER
TREEFOLK
VOODOO QUEEN
WEREWOLF
WIND-UP SKULL
WITCH
WOLFMAN
ZOMBEAN
ZOMBIE KING
ZOMBIE POTATO

From Donovan Scherer, the creator of Fear & Sunshine and other all-ages adventures into weird worlds of monsters and mischief comes this chilling bestiary known as Creature of the Week.

Through a peculiar and sometimes inaccurate process of democracy, these strange creatures were voted for by even stranger "human beings" across the social media platforms of intergalactic publishing empire, Studio Moonfall.

By following (but not in a way that would be considered stalking) on various internet channels, you may find an opportunity to help be a deciding factor in the future weeks of creature victory decisions.

You can visit our current (~2019 A.D.) Earth-base in Wisconsin or find us in cyberspace at www.studiomoonfall.com.

Please note:
If you happen to come across a blade-weilding cat in these pages, his name is Merder Ketten and he means you no harm.

BIGFOOT

BUSINESS SHARK

CHUPACABRA

DANCIN' KRAKEN

DONKEYCORN

GHOST

GRAVEMOTHER

HODAG

JERSEY DEVIL

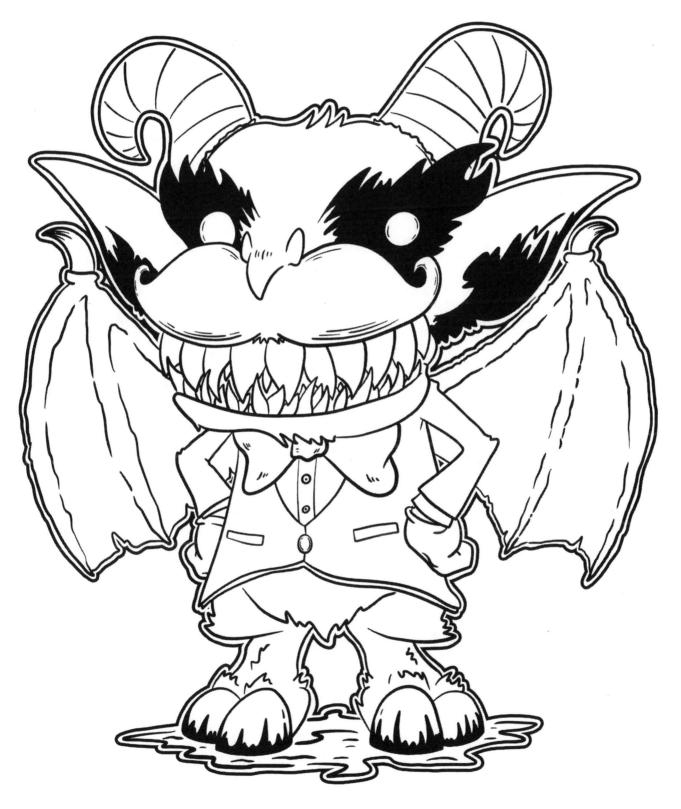

KRAMPUS

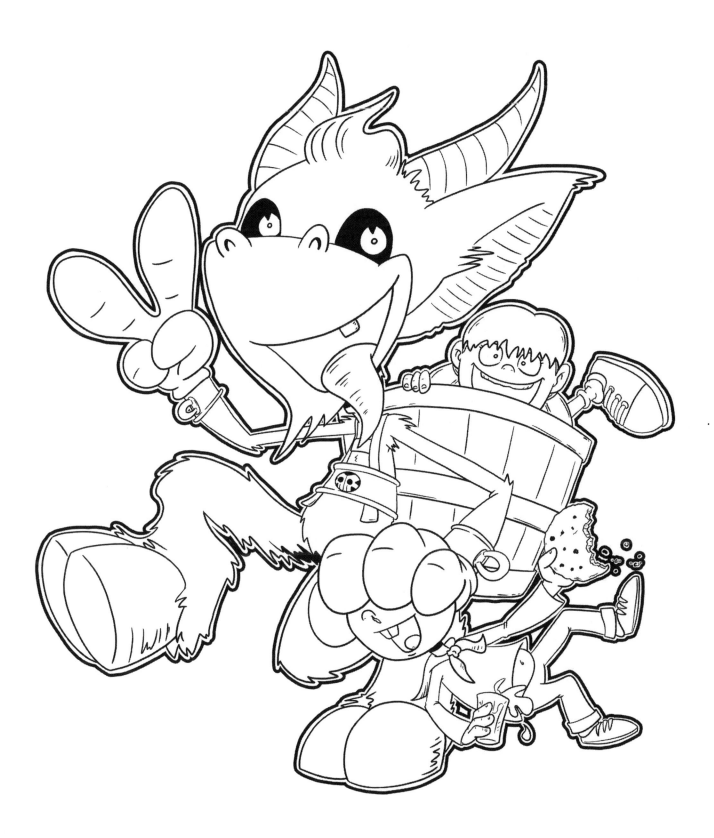

LOCH NESS MONSTER

MARI LWYD

MELVIN

MERMARK

MOTHMAN

MUMMY

NOSFERATU

OLD MAN WINTER

PIZZA OF BADNESS

PIZZA OF GOODNESS

PUGGERFLY

PUMPKIN KID

SALAMBEAU

SANDWITCH

SANTATHULHU

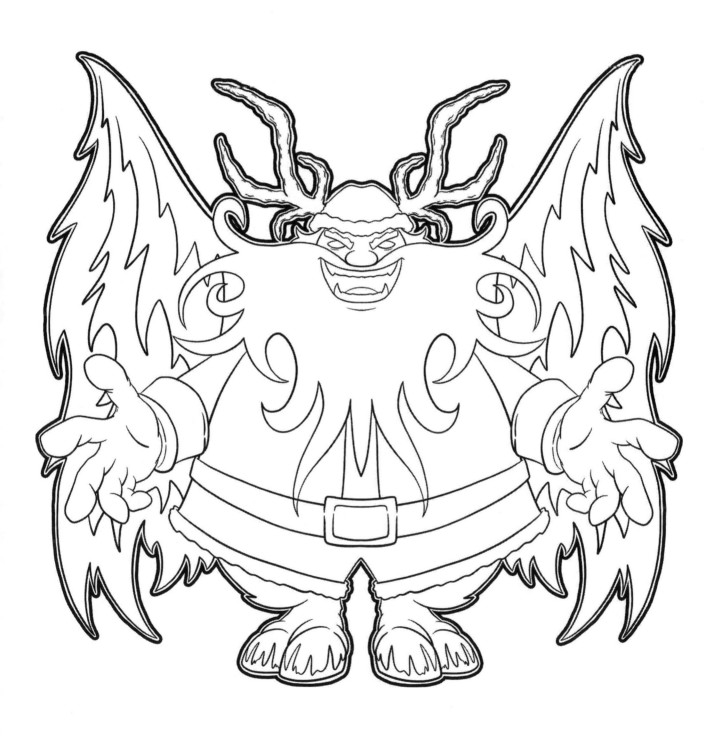

SHRUNKENHEADS

S'MORES

SPRING BABBY

TACO DOG

THE MOON

TOOTH FAIRY IMPOSTER

TREEFOLK

VOODOO QUEEN

WEREWOLF

WIND-UP SKULL

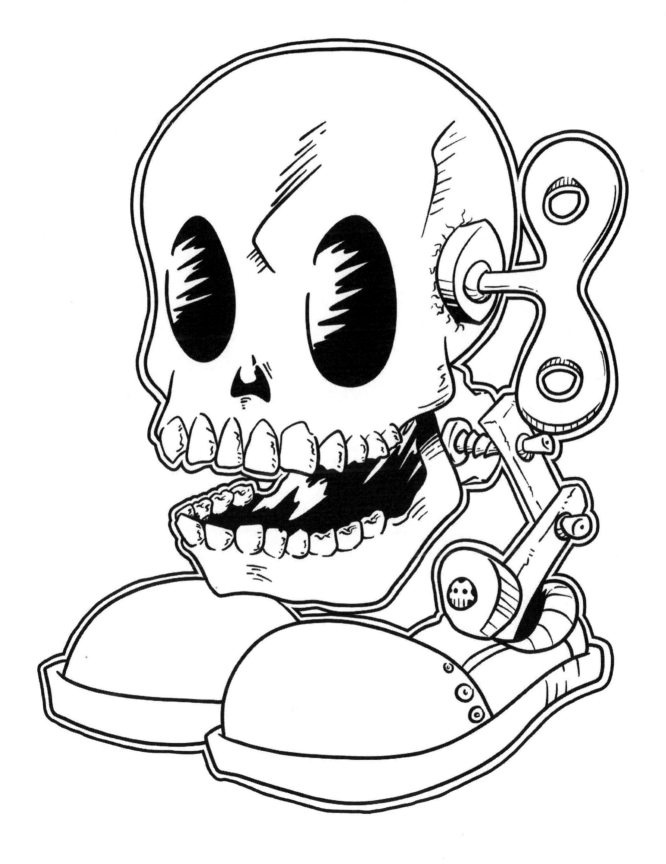

WITCH

WOLFMAN

ZOMBEAN

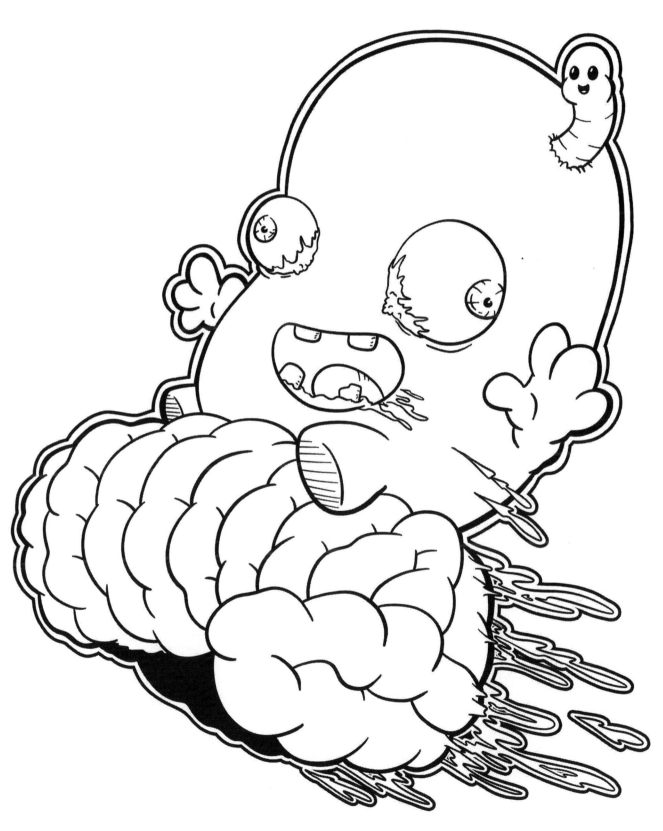

ZOMBIE KING

ZOMBIE POTATO

WHO'S YOUR MONSTER?

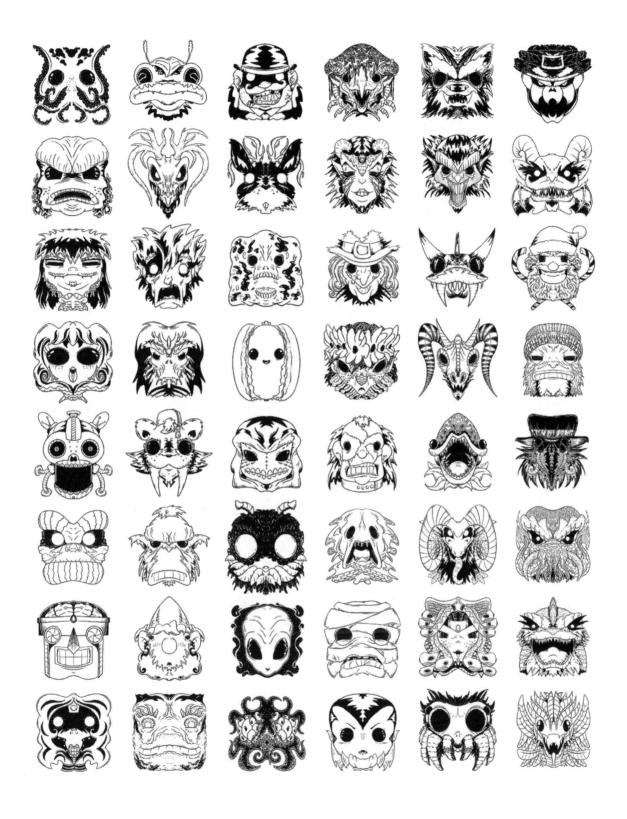

Get Your Favorite Creature on T-Shirts, Hoodies, and Journals at:

WWW.STUDIOMOONFALL.COM/AMAZON

For more all-ages adventures in horror, fantasy, and science fiction
by Donovan Scherer, the creator of this book, please visit:

www.StudioMoonfall.com

Made in the USA
Lexington, KY
22 November 2019